Dedicat
Cora's Gran

Sharon	Connie	~~Curt~~
Becky 🦋	Rusty	Kim
Judy	Jeff	Kevin
Jeri	Jon	
Sandy	Eric	

and Great Grandchildren!
and all future babies ♥

Jake Manu Holly PeTes PeTerson

allyse age 8

♡ Riley age 1½

EMLY

HEART WORLD
I ♡
Love is in the ...

Sarah Manu David KYLE Wo

♥ ♥
Bree Bunting (Samantha Age 3 mo.)

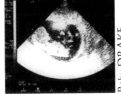

Baby DRAKE

Photogapher:
LB Photo
170 PRESTWICK POINTE
5250 E. U.S. Hwy. 36
Avon, IN 46122

Illustrations/Drawings by
Jon M. Jones, Amber M. Jones

Jewelry Designs by
Susan R. Jones
© 1997 Vintage Pin Studio

Before We Begin, Let Me Introduce You To Cora Louise

A little red-haired girl named Cora Louise Tyler was born in 1910 on a farm in the heartland of Indiana. Halley's Comet passed through on May 8th that year. William H. Taft was the president. The Campfire Girls and Boy Scouts were founded. Ten pounds of potatoes cost 17¢. The Secret Garden was published, and ladies were leafing through a new magazine called Womens' Wear Daily. Let Me Call You Sweetheart was a hit song. Times were a bit different. . . a little slower, and yet, families were very much the same.

I invite your family to take a pleasant journey back in time and enjoy the UNEXPECTED ADVENTURES of a little girl growing up in Indiana. . . and also take a peak at some interesting regional history.

Now, get snuggled into a comfortable chair. Get a little one on your lap if you have one handy. . . or maybe you prefer a cup of tea. . . ENJOY!

Trouble Upstairs

Cora Louise and her sister loved to play house. They played for hours in their big upstairs bedroom.

The sounds of Summertime in the country drifted in through the open window. The lace curtains moved gently to make way for a welcome breeze.

Their home sat up on a hill with big maple and oak trees shading the lawn.

They could look out the window and see their Father, with the big brown horses working across the field. They could hear the comforting sounds of their Mother cleaning downstairs. This was long, long ago. . . before there were TVs, or fast food restaurants, or videos, or shopping malls. There was no electricity in the beautiful farm home. Cora Louise's Mother washed all the family's clothes by hand and hung them on a line to dry in the sunshine. She cooked on a stove that was heated with wood and Oh-Oh-Oh what good food they had! Also, when it was dark, Cora Louise's Mother and Father lit lamps to light the house. The lamps were filled with lamp oil.

When Cora Louise and her sister went to
bed, their Mother took a wooden match
from a box on the shelf and lit a little lamp
that sat on their bedside table. After the
girls were snuggled in their bed, she blew
out the lamp. The hushed night sounds
came in the slightly opened window along
with a breeze so gentle it felt like a feather

on the girls' cheeks. Cora Louise and her sister would soon be fast asleep.

NOW, on this particular day, as Cora Louise and her sister were playing house, they made a very QUICK DECISION that since they were pretending to be grown-up, they could light the little lamp and say it was bedtime! Oh, yes, they knew they were NEVER, NEVER, NEVER to touch the matches. . . but it would be alright, they thought.

Oh, what fun! They lit the lamp with a long wooden match from the cardboard box upon the shelf. They climbed on the fluffy bed and pretended to sleep. Then they rolled and giggled and jumped, and then . . .OH NO! Something QUITE UNEXPECT-ED happened! The little lamp fell to the floor. The lamp oil spilled, and the fire flared up to the bedspread.

The girls screamed and their Mother dashed up the steps and quickly jerked the spread off the bed and stomped out the fire. Cora Louise and her sister were very scared. Their eyes were big, and they hung onto each other tightly because they knew they had done a very dangerous thing.

Their Mother took the white spread and waved it out the open window. Their Father saw the white spread from the field. He knew that was a sign that meant they needed help. He unhitched a horse and hurried as fast as he could through the field and up the hill to the house.

As he ran up the steps, two at a time, he could smell the smoke. He soon knew what had happened.

With his hands on his hips, he looked down at his little girls. Cora Louise's red, curly hair was disheveled, and it tumbled down over her face. He told them to sit on the bed, and he went downstairs. They sat still as little mice, wondering what their punishment would be.

When their Father returned, he had a rope which he promptly wrapped around his little girls and around the headboard of the bed.

He pushed his straw hat back on his sun burned head, looked sternly at them and said, Now, that should keep you girls out of trouble for the rest of the day! Shaking his head, he returned to his work in the field, and their mother returned to her work with an ever so slight trace of a smile.

The girls sat very still for a few minutes thinking about what had happened. Then they wiggled and wiggled and climbed out of the rope. They played VERY quietly the rest of the afternoon!

OH, by the way, they never bothered the matches again.

WANT TO KNOW MORE?

Would you like to know how old
Cora Louise was when this story
took place?

Do you want to know who was
President then?

Would you like to know Cora Louise's
sister's name ?

Turn to page 27.

The Big, Big Hill

The first grade was an exciting time for Cora Louise. She hopped and skipped down the grey steps of the family's big white farm house and hurried toward the path that led to her two room school. Her bright red hair shone in the early morning sun and her curls bounced as she swung her red lunch pail. She thought about how good her lunch would taste. Her Mother had packed a chunk of bologna in between two slices of home baked bread. It was wrapped

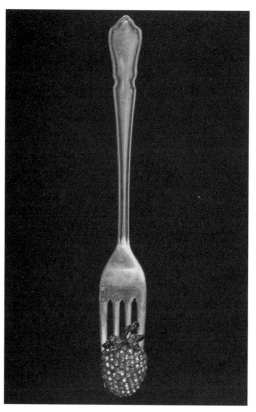

in waxed paper and held shut with a toothpick. She also had a red apple from Grandad's apple tree, and, best of all, a thick slice of chocolate cake with fudge icing with a bright red strawberry on top!

All the children brought their lunches to school. There were no cafeterias or vending machines. They ate their lunches at their desks, then they went out to play in the school yard.

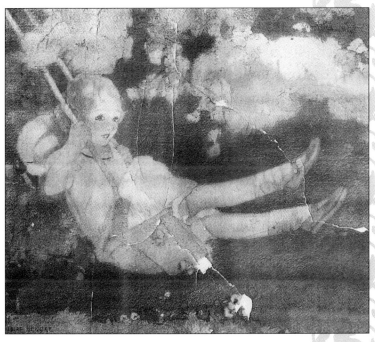

This is a print of a watercolor picture that hung in the old Pittsboro Elementary School where Cora's children and several Grandchildren attended.

The restrooms were outside in little buildings called outhouses.

A neighborhood girl who was older than Cora Louise waved and joined her for the long walk to school.

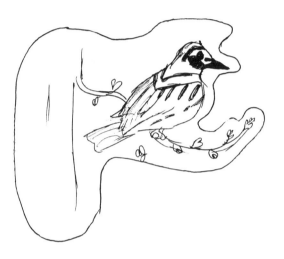

Cora Louise liked to walk with a friend. The crunching of the leaves under their feet, and the happy singing of the birds from above filled the warm, late summer air with just a trace of Fall.

Cora Louise was always in a hurry, and this morning was no exception. She ran ahead and came to the BIG, BIG HILL. She made a QUICK DECISION to take a short cut and run down the BIG, BIG HILL! So down she ran! Her little feet went faster and faster until something

QUITE UNEXPECTED happened . . .
Cora Louise tripped over a rock and down
she rolled and tumbled to the bottom of the
BIG, BIG HILL! Her red lunch pail flew
one direction. Her shiny red apple flew
another. Her bologna sandwich flew yet
another, and her chocolate cake with the
fudge icing and red strawberry on top flew
straight up in the air, never to be seen again.

Cora Louise's friend came running to help.
She brushed the dirt and leaves off her blue
cotton dress, straightened her curly red hair
and re-tied her big satin bow.

They rescued her red lunch pail but her
lunch was ruined.

Did Cora Louise cry and want to go back
home? Oh, no, for you – see . . .

she always had a smile, even when something quite unexpected happened. Cora Louise was always ready for an adventure, and she made the best of any situation.

So, off the two friends went, hand-in-hand to school on that September morning so long, long ago.

Oh, by the way, do you think Cora Louise had to go without lunch that day? Of course not! Her friend shared her lunch.

Also, Cora Louise didn't take the shortcut down the BIG, BIG HILL again. .

WANT TO KNOW MORE?

Would you like to know what year this story took place?

Would you like to read more about Cora Louise's school?

Find out what happened to Cora Louise's house.

Turn to page 33.

The Very Short Visit

At Cora Louise's house, Sunday afternoons were a time for visiting with friends and family. It was a time for children to run and play tag or hide-and-seek on the green lawn. It was a time for big people to sit on the white front porch and eat bowls of homemade ice cream with long silver spoons and sip lemonade from tall clear glasses.

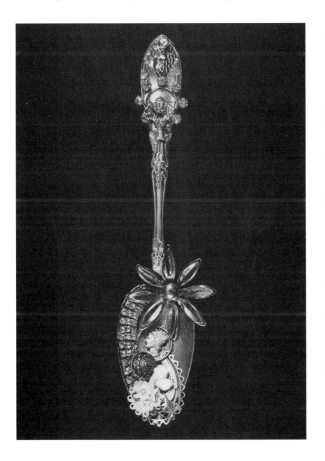

The men leaned back in wooden porch chairs, rolled up their white shirt sleeves and unbuttoned their starched collars. They talked in deep voices about farming, politics and the weather. The ladies fanned themselves with pleated paper fans and chatted about gardening and cooking and fussed over Cora Louise's new baby brother.

Cora Louise was growing up, and she enjoyed sitting and listening to the ladies for awhile, but not for too long. She always ended up going to play games with her sisters. She and her older sister now had two little sisters and a new baby brother!

Well, on this particular Sunday afternoon, Cora Louise's Aunt and Uncle came to visit. They had no children and loved to watch the little girls laugh and play.

The big people visited and had a fine time. All too soon, it was time for Aunt and Uncle to leave. They asked if Cora Louise could come home with them for a few days. Why, Yes! Her parents thought it was a fine idea. They knew that Aunt and Uncle must get lonely without any sweet children, and they were sure Cora Louise would brighten their lives! Also, Cora Louise was a very good worker, and she could help Aunt work in the vegetable garden, clean house, or roll out tasty homemade noodles!

Cora Louise climbed into the back seat of Aunt and Uncle's car. She held her bag with an extra dress, a night gown and her hair brush, on her lap. Off they went down the country road toward Aunt and Uncle's farm. Cora Louise felt proud to be going off on an adventure. She held her pretty head high and her red hair bounced as they rode over the winding gravel road.

Well, the next day at Aunt and Uncle's house, Cora Louise was outside when she had a VERY UNEXPECTED strange feeling. . .Aunt and Uncle were very nice. . .a bit stiff, but that was because they didn't have any children. Here there was no one to play with, no swing hanging from the tree, and everything was so quiet. Cora Louise began thinking about home. . . about her sisters and her new baby brother, her Mother and Father and all the good smells of their kitchen.

Suddenly, Cora Louise didn't want to be at Aunt and Uncles'. She wanted to be home. She made a QUICK DECISION to run and hide. She ran into the big, red barn. She climbed up the ladder to the hay mow. She stayed there and hid because she wanted to go home. She didn't hear Aunt and Uncle calling her. She didn't know they were worried and looking everywhere for her.

The Hayloft where Cora hid.

(Amber)

Finally, after what seemed like a very long time, Uncle came up the hay mow ladder and saw Cora Louise hiding in the hay.

Uncle promptly put Cora Louise in the front seat of the car. Uncle quickly put the bag with the extra dress, nightgown and hairbrush into the back seat, and off they went, back to Cora Louise's parents' farm. When they arrived, Uncle opened the door for Cora Louise, handed her the bag, spoke briefly to her parents and quickly headed back toward his farm. Cora Louise was so happy to be home! And as she looked up at her smiling parents, she could see they were happy too!

After that adventure, whenever Aunt and Uncle came to visit, they all had a fine time. But when it was time for them to go, they said their good byes, patted Cora Louise on the head, waved and drove home ALONE!

WANT TO KNOW MORE?

Would you like to know where Aunt and Uncle Lived?

Do you know how much Uncle's car cost?

Do you want to know what year it was?

Turn to page 41.

Evelyn, Cora, Edgar & Betty
Taken about in the early 1940's

Cora and Betty – around 1913

Cora, Nellie & Betty

*Cora Louise & Ralph Marshall
on their Wedding day*

*Cora Louise (with hair bow) with her Grandparents,
Tom & Nancy Ellen Tyler,
her parents, Ethel (with Sister Nellie)
& Ellis (with Sister Betty).
This was taken at the home
which stood at 56th & Potters Pike.*

This classic photograph of Cora
was taken in the early 1930's.

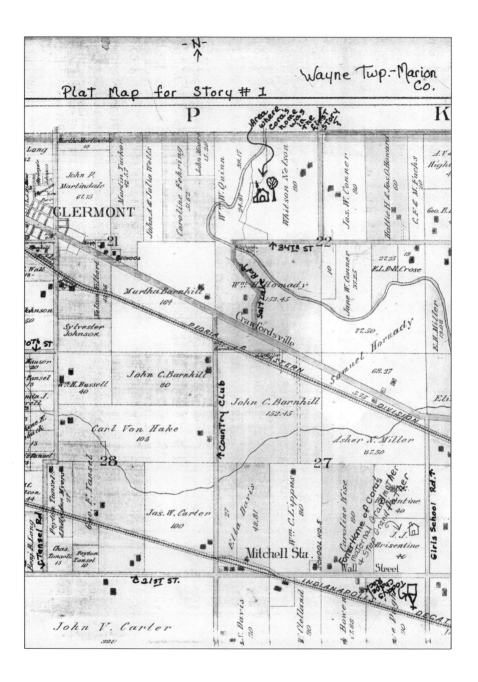

Memorabilia Surrounding "Trouble Upstairs"

This story took place about 1914. Woodrow Wilson was President. Cora Louise was around 4 years old. She, along with her older sister, Betty, and her parents, Ellis and Ethel Tyler, were living on a farm located in the winding, northwest part of Wayne Township in Marion County in Indiana. The exact location of the farm was the northeast corner of 34th Street and Dandy Trail. The farm extended East on 34th Street past the areas which are today's Eagles Landing and Marabou Mills communities. The farm extended on Dandy Trail north to include today's Trophy Club community. The original house stood on the hill which you can see as you enter Trophy Club. The original house was still standing until just a few years ago when the land was developed into housing. The house stood vacant for many years and had been, ironically, damaged by fire. As you look up from Dandy Trail, you can see the large trees and can visualize the white farm house standing there. The fields below could have been easily seen from the windows.

In 1914 W. 34th Street was hardly more than a path, and Dandy Trail was just a gravel road and not yet known as Dandy Trail. It must have seemed very far away from Indianapolis.

Here's an interesting note. . . one of Cora's granddaughters, Becky, lived for several years in one of the communities located on part of the original farm.

Many older people (older than me, that is) have told me they learned to drive up and down 34th Street because it was a remote area. It's for sure it was not patrolled in those days or they may have encountered the same brief, yet expensive, visit I had recently with a gentleman in a brown uniform who beckoned me to pull over because he was curious to know if I knew how fast I was going. The farm ground along 34th Street, along with the well-known Fox's Orchard has given way to lovely residential living, much of which has been brought to life under the supervision of Cora's builder son, Ken.

Three landmark houses still remain on 34th Street between Dandy Trail and High School Road, The Shockley home, The Nail home and the Skeeter home, which sits proudly in the center of Summerfield South community. The Dreyer estate between 34th and 38th

Streets is an impressive area of beautiful apartment communities with a winding, wide, tree-lined parkway leading to the welcome, new Target, Marsh Center on 38th Street. The long-awaited North Wayne Elementary School campus now sits in the shadows of yesterday's cornfields and is a true asset to children and the neighborhood. As Dandy Trail cuts its familiar way from Crawfordsville Road toward W. 38th Street, many local fisherman will fondly remember the old Dandy T fishing hole that is now home to The Islands Community.

West 38th Street, which divides Wayne and Pike townships, was a quiet road known as Maple Street, I am told. As late as the 1960's, huge farms and stately farm homes dominated West 38th Street in the area of the Cracker Barrel. The whole region was virtually rural to the little Eagle Creek Airport at the corner of 38th and Dandy Trail. The State of the Art Airpark has survived and thrived amid the growth. Another interesting business that has survived is the Eagle Creek Animal Clinic which began years ago as a small emergency care clinic and seemed to nearly disappear as housing began to surround it. It held its own, expanded and seems to have taken root among the mature trees. Its design, though remodeled, is still reminiscent of the prairie architecture of the 1950's and early 1960's.

It is a welcome and caring haven for all the
pets that now call this area home, too!

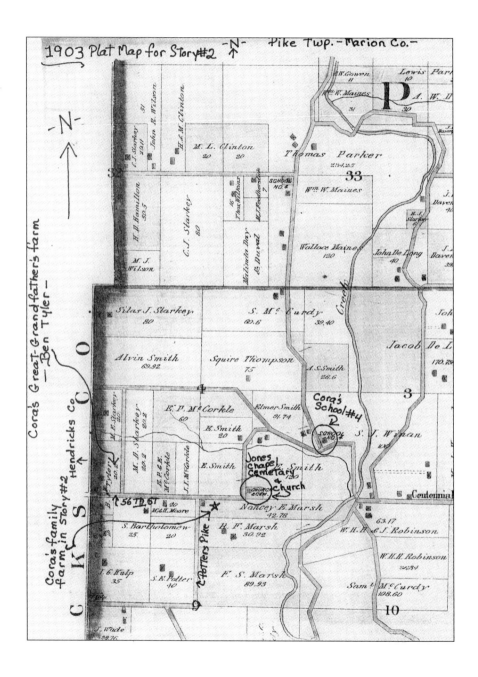

1903 Plat Map for Story #2   Pike Twp. - Marion Co. -

-N-↑

Cora's Great-Grandfather's farm — Ben Tyler —

Hendricks Co.

Cora's family farm in Story #2

-N-↑

Cora's School #4

Jones Chapel Cemetery & Church

← Potters Pike

Interesting Tidbits About "The Big, Big Hill"

This adventure took place in 1916 in Pike Township, Marion County, Indiana. The Pike Township community is steeped in a rich historical heritage. It was, at that time, a remote area of N.W. Marion County, far away from the city of Indianapolis. It was a place where many of Indiana's earliest settlers chose to call home. There were (and still are) grain and dairy farms and areas of rolling horse farms. Many prominent people of that time chose Pike Township in which to establish hide-away-homes secluded among the lovely landscape. Many of the early influential families have streets and roadways that bear their names. You may pass them every day; Marsh Road, Moller, Potter's Pike, Moore, Rodebaugh, Connarroe, Fishback, Reed and Guion just to name a few. Century old homes of beautiful architecture can still be seen as you travel through the township.

The exact location of the Tyler family farm at this time was on the S.E. corner of 56th St. and Potters Pike. The home sat up on the hill, with fruit trees growing on the slope toward Potters Pike. This ground, as you can see on the old plat map, was passed down to Cora Louise's Father by his Mother's family. Note the Marsh name on the plat. Quite sadly, the lovely home was destroyed in the tornado of 1948. Today a beautiful home sits in the same spot. Also, note the Tyler plot West on 56th Street. This was Ben Tyler's ground, Cora's Father's Grandfather's farm. Many branches of the Tyler family were rooted in this neighborhood. Some of the Tyler Aunts and Uncles that we have pictures of were Frank, Wallace, Ella Turpin, Mattie Trout, and Bill.

Cora's Father was Ellis Tyler, who was the only child of Tom Tyler and Nancy Ellen (Marsh) Tyler. Tom's father was Ben Tyler. The Tylers have been traced back to include our 10th president, John Tyler, who was from Virginia and was from the Whig Party and served from 1841-1845.

The Jones Chapel Church and Cemetery is another interesting landmark in the immediate area. You will see it just East of Potters Pike on the North side of 56th Street just West of the Eagle Creek Reservoir bridge. The tiny church was originally a Methodist Episcopal denomination, and, according to Cora's Great Uncle Bill Tyler, the church became non-denominational around 1936-37. The cemetery, which was established in 1841, is a resting place for many of the area's first settlers, including many members of the Tyler family. Lovely memorial services were held each May in the quaint country church. The Jones Chapel Church was destroyed in the tornado of 1948, in the same fury of nature that also destroyed the Tyler Family home. The foundation of the church can still be seen at the North edge of the cemetery.

The school Cora Louise attended, the very school she was on the way to when she tumbled down the hill, was #4. Cora remembers her teacher was Omega Pollard. It was located in the area of N. 56th Street and Dandy Trail. Dandy Trail continued North into what is now Eagle Creek Park and weaved gracefully through the tranquil countryside. The school, you can see on the plat map, is marked #4 and is now resting deep under the reservoir.

This particular school was one of 12 schools in the district, according to records I could find. It was a brick structure with 2 rooms and an auditorium. Many classic plays were presented in this auditorium for the entertainment of the community. After Cora graduated from Brownsburg High School in 1929, she was invited back to be in several plays in the #4 School's auditorium. People came from all over the area to enjoy the elaborate productions, and tickets were as much as 25¢.

Cora also remembers a covered bridge on 56th St. over Little Eagle Creek. It was under that bridge that her sister, Betty, was baptized.

Also, note on the plat map that what we know as 56th St. is labeled Centennial Road.

Dandy Trail has a fascinating history. Today's Dandy Trail winds from Crawfordsville Road to 56th Steet which borders Eagle Creek Park and is just West of the Indianapolis Colts Complex. Although the area is densely populated now, it remains an aesthetic drive and is a favorite of joggers and bicyclists who enjoy being treated to a panoramic view of Eagle Creek, whether it's a dazzling array of brightly colored sails of the boats of summer or the magnificent display of the blazing colors of fall. The sight of brown-eyed deer grazing alongside the roadway is common-place. The handsome homes that have been built along the way blend harmoniously with the remains of yesterday.

Dandy Trail was developed because of the

popularization of the motor car. There was an outcry from touring car owners for a pleasure route through the country that would be enjoyable, yet not so far away from home that they would get lost. Dandy Trail was laid out using existing gravel roads to encircle the city of Indianapolis. It was 88 miles in length and was, in fact, the city's first beltway! At its completion, they were hard-pressed for a name. The manager of the Hoosier Motor Club had been instrumental in the design, and he always had his little show dog with him, a black Pomeranian, named Dandy. They all agreed Dandy would be a fitting name, so, all along the route there were wooden markers bearing the name Dandy Trail and a silhouette of the perky little Dandy dog!

Mayor Charles Jewett formally accepted the trail at a ceremony in University Park in Indianapolis in 1920 and Dandy was in attendance. The Trail could be reached from any main highway in Indianapolis.

The last segment of the trail wound through Western Pike Township with a getting on or off point at Traders Point. Today, one of the most scenic sections now lies silently at the bottom of Eagle Creek Reservoir.

In the late 1950's, when my KW and I were dating, the most fun thing to do on a lazy,

hazy, summer afternoon was to get a pizza pie from the new Pizza Inn on Lafayette Road and drive down Dandy Trail, pull over to one of the picnic tables that were placed here and there along the Trail, and eat the marvelous pizza, enjoy the scenery, and dream of our futures. Many young people of that unforgettable era had their first taste of the heavenly, spicy food of the Italian Gods under the loving supervision of Papa Joe Haboush. Papa Joe's is still nestled in the same location and is now serving third generation Italian food lovers.

Life is interesting, isn't it?

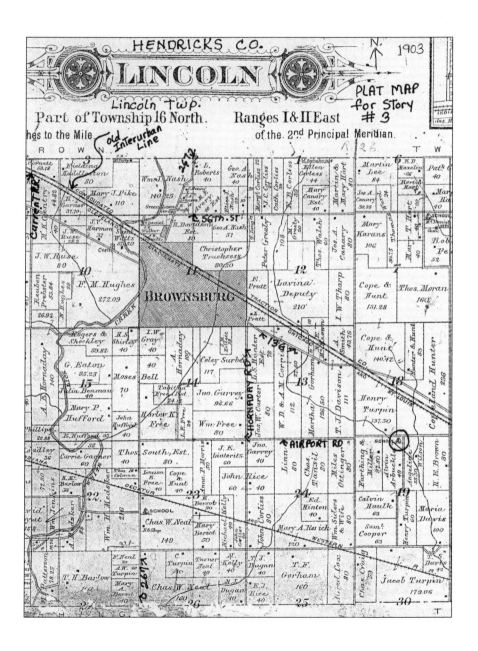

MIDDLE

Sparks' Cemetery

Current R.R.

Old Interurban Line

Hendricks Co.

N

T W

Jas. P. Reynolds
John Holloway 153.95

Mary E. Smith 62.36
Henry E. Holloway

David W. Holloway 30.27
Eliza A. Arbuckle 40

Mary E. Smith &
Henry E. Holloway 80

Jonathan P. Lauder 35.50
Wm. Spicklemeyer, Et.

Angeline Weddle 40

J. M. Hough Lauder & Herring 80

Jas. Isaac Tharp

Swnh. J. George 80

Alexander Arbuckle 140

Adam Beeman 80

T. J. Sandusky 120

Frank P. Marvel 80

John W. Jerry Metts Holloway Carter 42.91

Geo. D. Springer 44.40

H. A. Leonard 50

Frances Garner 76

John W. Martin 80

T. & J. Tharp 40

Thos. Tarpy 30

John Collins 80

Richard L. McDaniel 55

Nancy Tarpy 80

Iraac McDaniel 80

Sarah Lauder 100

Jonathan P. Lauder 60

Sumon Enllett

Thos. Cummins

Phillip Herring 60

Oliver Smith 79

Anna Phillips

M. E. Thos. J. Watson 60

A. W. School

Phillip Herring 60

Edward F. Nash 31.13

Frances Mildred Garner Garner 59 O.D.

C.C. McDaniel 44
C.C. Garner 70

Andrew S. Garner .96

Theo. P. Garner 80

Thos. J. Nash

Alice A. McDaniel 80

Susan Irwin

Thos. Cummins Everson

B. & J. Follmayer 27.76

Susan R.

Martin Sarah Mullen Irwin 40

Regan McClain G. A.

Jonathan McDaniel 63

Jas. W. Phillips 80

Alex. Phillips 39.35 John Kinner

Patrick Johnson

Higgins Alva Warren

Kate Walsh

Mary A. Eaton 80

Chas. C. Garner & Wife 80

Wm. P. Davison 80

Ed. Denton 40

White

Wm. Hopkins, Est.

M. J. Collins 80

Charling Hessian

Isaac McDaniel 63

Malinda E. Sandusky 80

Emma V. Warren 80

Wm. Budd Warren 60

Chas. Hessian 56

John R. Garner 59.50

Albert T. Garner

Martin Dwby

Mary A. Gibbs 150

Grant Arbuckle 159.50

Ellison Arbuckle 51

Hannah Coffman, Est. 105.78

Elizabeth Shoemaker Beard 160.83

Annabetta Beard 344

John Wonnell 68

John Everett Est. 80

W.E. Everett 40
Alice A. Everett

L.B. Lawler

J.J. Lawler

Susan Denny, Est. 37.50 40

J. M. Stigler 40

Wm. Kinney 40

D.S.M.

Anna Bridget Dugan Dugan 40 40

Timothy Quinn 94.83

A.M. Lee 80

John Hogan 95

John Lee, Est.

Harriet & Prott L.b. Lawler

Jas. M. Lawler 63.96

Daniel Tawdong 53.95 John Argoyle 40

John Kinney 69.50

Hirst

Martin Hirst

Stephen Maloney 30

Mary Maloney 40

John Collins

J. Hogan

John Lee, Est.

P. Hogan 78.49

Chas. R. Jowdan 40

Timothy L. Quinn 127

Thomas Maloney 40

James Hogan

John Lee

John Lee, Est. 66.66

P. Hogan

James Hogan Harp

Joseph Highlshin

James Hogan 160.63

Burd Beck

J. T. Dickerson 30

253.82

M DDLE

Facts About "The Very Short Visit" and Events Beyond

The year was 1923. Cora Louise was about 13 years old. Calvin Coolidge was the president. The car that Uncle and Aunt drove, if it was new, probably cost about $300.00.

The Aunt and Uncle in this story were Cora's Aunt Elva and Uncle Dory Evoy. Dory was Cora's Mother's brother.

Uncle Dory and Aunt Elva lived on a farm North and East of Brownsburg in the rich farming community of Brown Township. Aunt Elva was an Arbuckle, a prominent, well-known early family of Brownsburg. Note on the plat map, the name Arbuckle appears on many plots of ground, including what is now Brownsburg's lovely town park, Arbuckle Acres.

By the time she took the quick trip home from Aunt and Uncles', Cora's family had grown to include, in addition to her older sister, Betty and herself, 2 younger sisters, Nellie and Evelyn and a baby brother, Edgar.

Her family now lived in the Brownsburg
area and Cora attended the Turpin School.
Note the school on the plat map of Lincoln
Township. One of Cora's Granddaughters,
Judy, now has a lovely home in this very
vicinity. Cora graduated from Brownsburg
High School in 1929.

Her sister, Betty �, married Buck Wilson ✿,
and they spent their lives in the Brownsburg
and Speedway areas. They had one daugh-
ter, Nancy Ellen. Cora married Ralph M.
Jones ✮ and they lived in the Pittsboro area.
They had four children, Ann, Carol, Ken
and Chuck. Cora still resides in Hendricks
County. Nellie ✮ married Floyd Bilbee and
lived in Speedway. They had 3 Sons,
Ronnie ✮, Larry, and Gene. Floyd remains
in the area. Evelyn ✮ married James
Lee and they lived in Franklin. They had 2
Sons, David and Dennis. James still resides
in Franklin. Edgar ✮ married Martha Ellis
and they lived in Speedway, then retired to
Brazil. They had 3 children, Tom, Bob, and
Ginny. Martha now lives in Hendricks
County.

Each raised their families with the same
wisdom, respect, tenderness, and humor
they had experienced from their families.
They have been blessed with many grandchildren and great-grandchildren. The lega-
cy of appreciation is deeply entwined in

each new generation. . . as it should be.

I believe there are times when we should loosen the reins on our lives and go into adventures that await us in this world for we all too often choose the familiar paths we have carefully mapped out for ourselves.

Remember: Life is full of Unexpected Adventures! ENJOY!

About
Cora Louise Tyler Jones

Cora has spent her adult life on a lovely
farm in Hendricks County. Although very
much involved in community and work and
church affairs, Cora's lifelong career has
been homemaking, in the true sense of the
word. She was married to Ralph M. Jones
for over 50 years, and together they raised
four children; Ann, Carol, Ken and Chuck,
while successfully operating their family
farm. Today, Cora lives comfortably amid
family and friends and still retains that
special sense of adventure!

Our Family Stories

Our Family Stories

Our Family Stories